LETTERS
FROM ITALY

Also written and illustrated by Leonard Everett Fisher

LETTERS
FROM ITALY

written and illustrated by
Leonard Everett Fisher

FOUR WINDS PRESS
NEW YORK

LIBRARY OF CONGRESS CATALOGING IN PUBLICATION DATA

Fisher, Leonard Everett.
  Letters from Italy.

  Summary: A saga of an Italian family's immigration to
the United States, their subsequent life, and the return of
one son to Italy during World War II.
  [1. Italian Americans—Fiction. 2. Italy—Fiction.
3. World War, 1939–1945—Fiction] I. Title.
PZ7.F533Le3   [Fic]   76–42462
ISBN 0–590–07408–3

Published by Four Winds Press
A Division of Scholastic Magazines, Inc., New York, N.Y.
Copyright © 1977 by Leonard Everett Fisher
Printed in the United States of America
Library of Congress Catalog Card Number: 76–42462
5   4   3   2   1   81   80   79   78   77

To my New Haven friends

LETTERS
FROM ITALY

I

Ristorante Capello

October 23, 1943

Friday

❧ *one* ❧

The sun had begun its afternoon descent from the near cloudless Connecticut sky. Its cool light caught the bottom of a red, white and blue service banner fringed with gold that hung inside the front-door window of Ristorante Capello. The blue of the banner was a single, lonely star. It told every passerby and patron that someone dear to Angelo Capello, the proprietor, had gone to war.

The banner was a common sight. By this Friday, October 23, 1943, ten million or more Americans had gone to war. Most of these millions were represented in hometown windows—coast to coast—by red, white and blue service banners with or without gold fringe.

From the first weeks in July and all through the hot summer, the surge of war had taken on a new dimension for Angelo Capello—an awareness that had not touched him since the day he left Naples sixty years ago, a boy not yet thirteen.

Now Angelo Capello could see the whole hellish nightmare in his head. The war had come to the land of his origins.

American and British armies had taken Sicily and invaded the mainland of Europe—Italy. Italy quickly surrendered and declared war on Germany, her former partner. Mussolini, the longtime Italian leader, fled from Italian retribution into the protecting arms of German troops. Naples fell to the American Sixth Army Corps. Soon, the terrible battles with Germany for the rest of Italy would begin. Meanwhile, the doomed Germans stayed, fought and made the Allied blood run free before they fell back inch by inch. It would take the tough Allied armies eight months of hard fighting to reach Rome, one hundred miles to the north—a little over twelve miles a month.

However proud Angelo Capello was of his only son, Vinny, now living or dying in his ancestral land—Angelo did not know which—the red, white and blue service banner fringed with gold was a poor substitute. In fact, Angelo could not be sure that Vinny was anywhere near the Italian peninsula. He just assumed it. Vinny had been in some fighting in North Africa during the spring. Angelo knew that. And now that American troops had moved on to Italy, Vinny had to be among them, Angelo reasoned.

"He's an experienced officer," Angelo would tell his cronies, "who happens to speak Italian. If I were Eisenhower that's what I'd do—send Vinny to Italy."

Angelo's only consolation—if it could be called that—was that his late and loving wife, Philomena, had passed from this world before she had to endure the agony of having her only son on some God forsaken battlefield, even if that battlefield was Italy.

"It would have killed her," Angelo often remarked. "Vinny will make it. He can take care of himself. But Philomena would have been a casualty. She would have worried herself to death. And the newspaper would say CAPELLO, PHILOMENA LOMBARDOZZI, KILLED IN ACTION."

⊰ *two* ⊱

A few inches from the service banner and also partially nipped by the falling sun was a carefully lettered sign:

CLOSED

WILL OPEN TUESDAY

OCT. 27

In another hour, sunlight would spread across the front of Ristorante Capello and envelop the entire east side of Olive Street, the heart of New Haven's Italo-American community.

Two skinny young sailors, one very tall, the other of average height, each gripping an overnight bag, shifted impatiently as they watched a postman shove some letters and bills through a shiny brass mail slot in the door of the restaurant. It was the day's second delivery.

"The old man's got some overseas mail this time around," the letter carrier said as he turned to leave. "Can I help you boys any? I'm an old navy man myself, you know. The big war. Subchasers and those four-stacker cans. Don't make the likes of them anymore."

"We're O.K., pal. Thanks just the same. We'll holler if we need you."

"You do that." The letter carrier nodded a few times and shuffled off, sorting a few pieces of mail for his next delivery. Partway down the street he stopped, waved, read a postcard meant for someone else and finally moved on.

The sailors quickly pressed against the window and peered through what space was left between the banner and the sign. Their view was disappointing. A narrow vestibule and another closed door—a windowless door—blocked any sight of the restaurant's vivid interior.

"Anybody home?" the shorter of the two sailors shouted as he all but shook the door off its hinges.

"Forget it, Sal. No one's home. The placed is closed. Can't you read?"

"Forget it! Are you crazy or something? Capello's never closes, no matter what! This happens to be the best spaghetti joint in town. They can't do this to me! I can't chase broads on an empty stomach. We've only got two days' liberty!"

"Come on, Sal. Let's go. We're wasting valuable time."

"Go where? I've been thinking about *carciofini alla Capello** for the past four months. Aah. What do you know anyway? You never had it so good until you hit navy apple butter and they gave you a pair of shoes."

---

* Artichoke hearts cooked in olive oil in a special Capello way.

(6)

"What about your folks? Maybe you ought to go home first and give your mama a break. We'll eat her *carci-o-fi-* or whatever you call it and then we'll chase broads."

"Iowa, you gotta be kidding. First of all, there are so many Fiores they don't even know I'm missing. Second of all—and I've told you this a thousand times—my mother and father are Italian but that doesn't mean mama can cook and papa can sing. They're Americans too, you know. Mama's spaghetti tastes like a loose ball of string dipped into a bottle of warm ketchup. And papa's basso profundo sounds like a sick elephant doing an imitation of Bing Crosby."

"I think you're crazy, Sal. Disrespectful, too."

"Listen, Iowa, I called home from the station when we got in. No one's home. And I know where they are. Mama is out hustling a poker or Mah-Jongg game. Papa is covering *bocce* bets all over New Haven. They never lose. The stakes are big. That's how come we Fiores eat out in style every day, every night, fourteen times a week. We eat cornflakes at home."

Sal Fiore hammered the door.

A handsome old leathery face framed by a cascade of silver hair parted right down the middle appeared at the window. A well-manicured hand flickered across the face holding the mail it had just picked up. The hand pointed to the sign and wigwagged a silent message: Go away!

"Mr. Capello. Open up. It's me, Sal. Sal Fiore. This is my buddy, Iowa. We've only got a couple of days. We're hungry."

The face, uncertain and blinded by the sun's glare exploding through the window, finally smiled in seeming recognition. Then it nodded as if to say, "How nice to see you" and once again flagged the message: Go away!

Sal stood his ground. "Mr. Capello. Please."

The old man gave in. After all, the Fiores were regular customers even though he did not think much of them. They were all cork-

(7)

screws so far as Angelo was concerned. Sal was one of them. But now he was a United States sailor. That was different. The door opened a crack.

"Welcome home, Salvatore. How's the war? Don't they feed you? Go home. Your mama and papa are waiting. You can come back on Sunday."

"Sunday! Why? What's going on? How come you're closed?"

"Be a good sailor, Salvatore. We have to fix the place up. Change the menu. Angelina's getting married Sunday. Angelina and Louis Bianchi from San Francisco. Nice boy. Private first class. Your mama and papa will be here. Bring your friend. Eat all you want. On the house. But Sunday, O.K.?"

"O.K., Mr. Capello. You win. Sunday. It'll be a tight squeeze. But we'll make it. We'll just catch a later train. Come on, Iowa, you hayseed. You heard what the *padrone* said. He's the boss. Scratch one broad—Angelina—and let's go. *Andiamo*."

Angelo did not hear the last crack about Angelina. He had already disappeared inside the restaurant.

"Who is Angelina?" Iowa wanted to know.

"His granddaughter," Sal responded. *"Bella! Bellissima!"* Sal rolled his eyes and kissed his own fingertips in a gesture of admiration for the wondrous Angelina.

✣ *three* ✣

Ristorante Capello was no run-of-the-mill "spaghetti joint" as Sal Fiore had put it. Sal knew that. It was just his way of talking tough now that he was in the navy. Sal was not born into the Italian life of New Haven, Connecticut, to reach the age of nineteen without having been schooled on the marvels of the restaurant's incomparable cuisine—*veramente Italiano*—authentic Italian.

Angelo Capello indulged in a lifelong dream when he opened the place back in 1914. He had already made a fortune as a building contractor in and around New Haven and needed a hobby. When he retired from his building business some years later, a rich man by anyone's measure, Ristorante Capello had already earned an enviable reputation among New England's gourmet diners. Now, no longer a hobby, Ristorante Capello was Angelo Capello's obsession.

Angelo spared no expense either in the building of the restaurant or in the old-world tone of its interior or in the quality of his varied menu.

The building itself was a rambling stone and stucco replica of some *palazzo* Angelo dimly remembered from his boyhood around Naples. Inside, the place was comfortable and full of Italian reminders. During the late 1920s and early '30s Angelo commissioned a number of talented students from the nearby Yale Art School on Chapel Street— none of whom were even faintly Italian—to decorate every square foot of wall space with brilliant, atmospheric scenes of Italy. Except for the one mural of the Bay of Naples, Angelo Capello had never seen any of it until they came to life on the walls of his restaurant: Venice's Piazza San Marco; the Ponte Vecchio in Florence; St. Peter's Square in Rome; the Leaning Tower of Pisa; and the Cathedral of Milan.

At one point, Angelo was going to add the "Sistine Room," a small-scale duplicate of the Vatican's Sistine Chapel in Rome where the Popes were elected. Although he had never seen it, Angelo could visualize the entire chapel in his restaurant—Michelangelo's *Ceiling* and *Last Judgment* and other authentic decorations. *Veramente Sistina.* Authentic Sistine. But World War II came and the art students of Yale went off to make maps and camouflage ships.

Only one wall remained to be finished. This was to be a monumental mural of Rome's Castel Sant' Angelo, a circular fortresslike tomb of Roman Emperors from Hadrian to Septimius Severus. Angelo Capello's ego could not be denied. But this too would have to wait. The artist had been drafted.

As for some equally important aspects of Ristorante Capello: The food was excellent; the service was personal and ingratiating. The chef and kitchen staff were the finest anywhere—the best-paid culinary craftsmen in New England.

Interestingly enough, none of this seemed to rub off on Angelo Capello: not his wealth; not his wide business contacts; not the depth of his self-education. Through it all he remained a straight-talking, plain man, however debonair in appearance he seemed to be. Angelo Capello treated everyone alike, the lowly and the mighty. He was generous almost to a fault. He expected nothing in return.

"This country took us in when we had nothing. I must give something back," he constantly reminded his children and grandchildren.

Above the cash register of Ristorante Capello were two framed letters thanking him for his contributions to the Democratic party. Both letters were on White House stationery. Both letters were signed "Franklin Delano Roosevelt." The first letter was addressed to "Dear Mr. Capello." The second letter was addressed to "Dear Angelo." By the time Angelo had received the second letter, he had already been to the White House and met the President of the United States. That was six years ago in 1937. It was the proudest moment of his life.

His lowest moment came some years before when Dutch Schultz, the notorious beer-baron racketeer, came to Ristorante Capello for nothing more than a fine dinner. Schultz had nine gun-toting henchmen with him and no reservation. With a flurry of quiet nervousness, Angelo found a suitable table and personally seated Schultz and his party. Angelo then retreated to the kitchen where he promptly fainted. When he came to, he had an ice bag on his head and Philomena was vigorously rubbing his wrists.

"Has he gone?" Angelo asked.

"Not yet," Philomena replied.

Angelo fainted again. This time he sagged in Philomena's arms. Dutch Schultz finally left but not without promising that he and his boys would return. He never did come back.

Now, war and age had caught up with Angelo Capello. He seemed to slip more readily into his own world of foggy memories and hazy heritage. He sprinkled his speech with more Italian idioms than he ever knew as an immigrant boy. In his younger days, when he was bright with ambition and all of America seemed to lie at his feet, Angelo was more Yankee in his outlook and pride than the Sons and Daughters of the American Revolution. And this despite his name, his restaurant, his community associations—the Sons of Italy, for one—his ethnic loyalties.

Lately, however, with a piece of him—his soldier son—in the land of the Capello beginnings, Angelo began to affect more Italian mannerisms than he realized. The interior appearance of his restaurant—unabashedly Italian—had worked its magic on him. Angelo Capello was slipping into a time machine, partly of his own making and partly engineered by the strategic coincidence of war.

⇘ *four* ⇙

Angelo sat down at the far end of the main dining room to keep out of the way of the bustling wedding preparations. Behind him was the Bay of Naples painted with startling realism. He spread the half-dozen pieces of mail on the table before him, removed his glasses from an inside pocket of his gray tweed jacket, blew on them, wiped them with a corner of the tablecloth, set them on his long straight nose and hooked them over his ears. Now he was ready to examine the still-sealed envelopes. Almost immediately Angelo noticed the two postage-free, overseas airmail envelopes.

"Vinny," he gasped and clutched one envelope in each hand.

Angelo did not tear either one of them open right away. Instead, he studied them carefully, turning each of them over and over in his shaking hands one at a time. Angelo's keen appraisal of the envelopes told him several things: the cancellation dates were weeks apart; the addresses were quite different from one another; and Vinny had been promoted from captain to major.

The earliest of the two letters was postmarked August 24. The return address indicated that Captain Theodore V. Capello was with Division Headquarters of the First Infantry Division in General George S. Patton's Seventh Army.

Angelo growled about "the army's lousy mail service." The letter had been written two months ago.

The more recent letter was postmarked October 19, only four days ago. Vinny was no longer with the First Infantry. Now he was Major Capello and assigned to Division Headquarters of the Thirty-sixth Division in General Mark W. Clark's Fifth Army.

Angelo did not need to know anything else. He did not want to know anything else. He knew exactly where Vinny had been and where he was now. The news reports told the story. The Thirty-sixth Division had been badly mauled all around Paestum in the Gulf of Salerno before it controlled the invaded beachhead. Now, according to the radio news, the Fifth Army was pinned down just north of Naples and south of the Volturno River. The worst was yet to come.

"*Dio mio!*" Angelo muttered to himself. "My God!"

❧ *five* ❧

Angelo neatly slit open with a penknife the letter postmarked August 24. The letter itself was dated August 19, two days after the Germans were driven from Sicily.

Dear Papa:

First things first. I am fine. Fit as a fiddle. I am sorry that you have not heard from me more often. I am sure that you read the papers and know the reason by now.

Sicily has fallen. It is no particular secret that my Division, the First Infantry, went ashore at Gela. Have you ever been there? Probably not. It doesn't matter. What a sad little place.

I spent a good deal of time talking to the local people from Gela to Messina. They didn't like the shooting. Who could blame them. Neither did I. Wherever I have gone people seem to be more relieved over the fact that Mussolini is gone—"finito Benito" you hear all over—than anything else. Right now I am happy that the fighting is over for me too—although I was comparatively safe most of the time. I am still here, on the island, however. That's no secret either.

How are you and everyone? Your mail has not caught up with me as yet. I'll tell you one thing. A little fettucine al doppio burro* alla Capello *wouldn't hurt. Army chow is army chow. Sicilian cooking might be something else again if they had any-thing to cook. There is plenty of wine around and it's not half bad.*

Stay well. Regards to all. Don't worry about me. I shall write again as soon as I am able.

Your loving son, Vinny

* Boiled noodles drowned in butter and cream.

⤳ *six* ⤶

Theodore Vincent "Vinny" Capello was the bright, rugged American promise of his father's dreams. The only bothersome spot in his otherwise perfect past, present and future was that he was a forty-year-old bachelor and getting older. This added up to an abominable waste in Angelo's productive views and plans. Vinny, a lawyer and onetime Ivy League athlete (Harvard '25—football, track and swimming) collected legal fees and women like rainwater.

"If you do not want to give me grandsons, Vinny," Angelo would constantly scold him, "then you should have become a priest to save yourself."

"You mean save you, Papa, from all the explaining you have to do. You know what, Papa? I think you are a little jealous."

"Jealous! Me! Jealous? Don't let your mother hear you say that!" And they both would laugh.

But no greater love had any son for his father than that shown by Vinny Capello one brisk autumn day at the Yale Bowl after having played his last game for Harvard against Yale.

Vinny, the best six-foot-two-inch End ever to come out of New Haven's Hillhouse High School and bypass Yale for Harvard, found himself down with the ball when the final whistle blew. Yale had won. Angelo, who had never gone to any college, but who, nevertheless, was a loyal Yale fan, was seated in his usual place on the Yale fifty-yard line deep in the late afternoon shadows below the press box.

Vinny tore across the field, his ripped crimson jersey fluttering like a flag in the wind. He ran into the stands where his father sat. Philomena was not there. She never went to football games, likening them to Nero's ancient, decadent, Roman gladiator combat. There Vinny presented the ball to his father in full view of seventy thousand roaring spectators. None of them knew exactly what was going on except that a misguided Harvard player was giving the game ball to Yale in some kind of a magnificent gesture that could only happen at The Game, the traditional title given every Harvard-Yale football contest.

Angelo almost cried. "You should have gone to Yale, Vinny," Angelo told his son right then and there. "But Harvard's not bad either—for a Capello." Father and son embraced to the delight of the picture-taking press. The whole sentimental story gushed on every sports page in the country the following day, but not without a small exaggeration.

"Harvard All-American gives game ball to *Yale* Dad."

"Now I feel like George Washington," Angelo dramatically announced to Philomena.

"Angelo, you are all mixed up. You are not the father of your country," she gently told him. "You are Angelo Capello, father of Caroline, Frances and," she added mockingly, "that big-shot son of yours, T. Vincent Capello, who still belongs in diapers."

Vinny Capello was the youngest of Angelo and Philomena's three children. Born in New Haven in 1903, Vinny was named in honor of Theodore Roosevelt, twenty-sixth President of the United States at the time. Vinny wanted no part of *Theodore* and chose to sign his name forevermore "T. Vincent Capello." Angelo did not care what Vinny did or did not do with "Theodore." It was on the record, on his birth and baptismal certificates. And that was that! Every so often Angelo would remind Vinny of his national responsibilities by calling him "Teddy." Vinny ignored him.

Vinny's sisters were older. But, like their brother, they too were named after someone in the White House at the time of their births.

Caroline, the eldest, was named for Caroline Harrison, wife of the twenty-third President, Benjamin Harrison. Caroline, whose chiseled good looks and grace demanded attention wherever she went, was the wife of New Haven banker August T. Palmieri. It was their daughter, Angelina, who was about to be married at her grandfather's church.

The beautiful and more delicate Frances, mother of four more daughters and wife of Hartford's incorruptible chief of detectives, Irishman Patrick J. Donnelly, was named for Frances Cleveland, wife of Grover Cleveland, the twenty-fourth American President.

This entire patriotic ritual—this thirst for Americanization—was Angelo's idea and passion. Dutiful Philomena never argued the point. However, both Angelo and Philomena were proud and grateful that their three children were the first Capellos anywhere to have been born in the United States of America.

Years later Vinny would often needle his father with the idea that had he and his sisters been born in Italy, they surely would have been named in honor of Giuseppe Garibaldi; Camillo Benso, the Count of Cavour; and Giuseppe Mazzini—or any of their wives and mistresses.

Angelo agreed and added that if his father and grandfather had the good sense to honor important leaders by including their names on the family tree, life would have been much better for all of them in Naples.

"And we would still be there. Right, Papa?"

"Right."

"Wrong. You would have stayed, Papa. Not me," Vinny told him.

To Angelo and Philomena Capello, Vinny's educational and athletic success was awesome if not something of a miracle.

"We came to America penniless and ignorant foreigners," Angelo lectured his family on the day Vinny graduated from Harvard. "We are not exactly penniless. And we are no longer ignorant foreigners."

America was a Capello paradise in Angelo's mind. It was not all that easy in the beginning. The streets were not paved with gold. No one knew that better than Angelo. He had paved a few of them himself—with asphalt—before he was sixteen years old. Yet, in spite of it, his good fortune seemed too easy, too quick.

On the night of Vinny's graduation he dreamed that the ghost of George Washington came to him and presented him with a bill for "services rendered."

"You were not here, Angelo Capello, when we pledged our lives and fortunes to make this country free. You have benefited greatly, Angelo Capello," the ghost solemnly intoned, "by the opportunities we made available to the likes of you. And so, Angelo Capello, you must pay for these opportunities."

Angelo awoke from his nightmare in a drenching sweat. He had no idea what the ghost meant. Had he not already paid plenty to be where he was? If the ghost of George Washington was not interested in hard cash, then what was it interested in? Was he, Angelo Capello, not a loyal, law-abiding citizen? Did he not properly name his children after important Americans? Did he not improve America with his buildings and restaurant and political contributions?

"You have no right to bill me," Angelo screamed at his dream.

Philomena was jolted awake. "What's wrong, Angelo?"

"Nothing. Go back to sleep."

Vinny went on to study law; graduated from the Yale Law School; passed the Connecticut bar exam and joined a New Haven law firm whose chief client was Capello Contractors, Inc. Still restless, Vinny quit the firm after a couple of years to be on his own. Angelo did not like the idea but he understood, having faith that one day his son would change his mind and return.

During the next decade Vinny developed a fine legal practice; watched his mother die; and spent a good deal of time spending his money with abandon.

(20)

One week after the Japanese attack on Pearl Harbor, Vinny Capello gave it all up. He secured an army commission and was assigned to the Judge Advocate General's Department, the army's legal branch, in Washington, D.C.

Vinny's fluency in Italian, however, made him more valuable elsewhere. By December 1942, Captain Capello was in North Africa. By the following March he was interrogating hordes of Italian war prisoners trapped by the Allied army along the Tunisian coast. In late June 1943, he was assigned to the G2 (intelligence) section, Division Headquarters, First Infantry. On July 10 he went ashore at Gela, Sicily. On August 25, Captain Capello was promoted to Major Capello and returned to Oran, Algeria, for reassignment to the Thirty-sixth Division.

On September 10, one day after the American Fifth Army's assault of the Italian mainland, Major T. Vincent Capello, divisional intelligence staff officer, stepped on the still bloody sands of Paestum, a once quiet resort town on the Gulf of Salerno. From there, he made his way to his divisional headquarters, now precariously doing its deadly business inside an ancient Greek temple.

ᘐ *seven* ᘒ

Dear Papa:

If you have been following the progress of the war (and I know that you have) you have already guessed that I am in Italy. You are right! Not only that, I am in Napoli!

Since I last wrote (a couple of months ago, I know, and I apologize for that—we have been very busy—I have received your letters, however), a few interesting things have happened. I have been

*transferred to the Thirty-sixth Division for reasons that I cannot
now explain. Also, I have been promoted. So when you write again,
take note of all the changes for the proper address.*

*Anyway, I have no way of knowing whether this is the Naples
you left behind or a newer Naples. Whatever it is, it's a mess.
The Krauts did a good job of destroying the whole port area before
they ran. I think they were sore because the Italians got out of the
war. They opened all the jails and let the hoods out to loot everything in sight.*

At the moment, there seem to be more paesani *in my Division than
in Naples. All of these half-starved locals are* innocenti. *When we
question them about Il Duce and the Fascisti, they all plead inno-
cent. Some even say they never heard of either. Others claim innocence by saying the Germans held them hostage or that they
were victimized. A whole country? Maybe so. Maybe not. They
think that I can understand and be sympathetic. I have instant
relatives all over the place. I cannot pass judgment. But after what
I have seen I find it difficult to be sympathetic. Understanding
perhaps. Understanding of their supreme stupidity.* Stupido!
Stupido! Stupido!

*It took us a long time to get here from Paestum, where we first
came in. The radio and papers must be full of what has been going
on. I wonder if anyone really knows. The fighting was more in-
tense than any one of us could have imagined. Africa wasn't bad.
Sicily had its moments. But this! Death and agony, ruin and rot
everywhere. What a God-awful price we are paying for Europe's
madness. Until now, my outfit has been in the middle of it, or so it
seemed. I'm O.K. tho'.*

*Italy may have surrendered, but it will be a long time before this
pitiful place knows any peace. Smiling Al* will see to that! The*

* Field Marshal Alfred Kesselring, German commander in south Italy.

(23)

Germans aren't going to quit too easily. In the end we will beat the living hell out of them but we shall pay, pay and pay some more. God help us! What a waste!

I can see Vesuvius as I write. A curl of smoke is climbing out of the crater. Maybe the old volcano will blow with the biggest bang yet.

I know there must be family here somewhere. We talked about it often enough. I wish I had paid more attention. Perhaps you could send me a list of some kind that could give me a starting point. Grandpa Luigi had brothers and sisters here. Somebody must know something. I only hope I am here long enough to find out.

I did remember one thing. The old church near the Piazza Carita, S. Liborio. I said Mass there last Sunday. It was the only time I felt I had been here before. I was overcome.

I am going to try and drive the short distance to Castellammare di Stabia. I passed by the town once but could not stop. I know that mama had two sisters there. Maybe somebody will know something.

In the meantime, regards to all.

Don't worry about me. I'm benissimo. *Take care of yourself.*

Your loving son,
Vinny

P.S. In case you are wondering, no one at S. Liborio knew of the whereabouts of any Capellos. But then again, I did not speak to everyone there. Some people I talked to, including a half-blind priest, were familiar with the name but could offer nothing more. I shall go back there again however. Something might turn up. I shall be optimistic.

❧ *eight* ❦

Angelo let the letter settle on the table. The low, frantic buzz of wedding preparations no longer seemed to flit around him. It floated in from afar, a jibberish, rising hum, swaying and shifting until it seemed to come out of the wall behind him. It circled his head and disappeared into the wall only to rise again out of the Bay of Naples.

Angelo turned and stared at the painting of his boyhood city. In that instant he exchanged one reality for another. Angelo came alive in the painting, mingling with the street noises of old Napoli. He was mesmerized by memories that held him fast and then flung him back to the Bay of Naples from whence he came.

Ciao, Angelo Capello. *Come va?* How are things?

II

Beginnings

September 24, 1870

Saturday

﹋ *one* ﹌

Angelo Capello dreamily strolled from the far end of the old, broken-down dock toward the sound and bustle of Naples. The sun was behind him, slipping faithfully downward in the western sky. He was barefoot—a well-scuffed shoe in each hand—unmindful of the coarse timbers of the dock. Being barefoot, which was most of the time, made him feel weightless and free, ready to fly in great circles like the screeching gulls above. Besides, being barefoot saved his shoes for more ceremonious occasions like weddings, funerals and birthdays. Today was Angelo's birthday.

"Your feet can take care of themselves," his mother, Madelena, never failed to remind him, "but your shoes are pure gold. Guard them well."

Angelo stopped to inspect some splinters imbedded in the balls of his feet. They weren't deep. Just annoying. He'd get them out later. Meanwhile, he tried walking stiff-legged, on the heels of both feet.

Angelo had spent the late afternoon at his favorite perch on the dock, squinting at the quiet sea. He was alone as usual. He had few friends. In a few minutes—if he could manage it—he would be off the dock, tend to his splinters and head for home.

All afternoon, there on the dock, like yesterday, the day before yesterday, and the day before that, the memory of his grandfather drifted in and out of his reverie. Angelo could hardly keep the old revolutionary out. They had been a special pair, those two. But now Piero Capello was gone. Angelo tried not to think about the accident.

He dodged a gaping hole in the planking. Enough was enough. His feet hurt and his legs felt like wood stilts. He sat down where he was —about midway on the dock—and began to rid himself of the pesky splinters.

Angelo was probably the only twelve-year-old in Naples who knew the meaning of the senseless, ageless racket that rose from the streets and assaulted his ears as he worked the splinters free. His grandfather, Piero Capello, saw to that part of his education. From the beginning of his life to the end, Piero was a patriot and loyal son of Italy and not much of anything else. He had soldiered in the armies that battled for Italian liberation. He had fought to free Naples from the French. He had become a policeman. He knew his city backward and forward, inside and out.

It was not that Luigi Capello—Angelo's father and Piero's son—did not know these things. He had heard it all before. Luigi was a quiet man who eked out a living fixing streets. He was more concerned over the fate of his own immediate family—his wife Madelena and their seven children—than the destinies of Italy. Luigi had one compelling notion. He wanted to get out of Naples and improve their lot. He did not have too much time for Angelo. Piero willingly took up the slack. And Angelo was a proud, eager listener of every tale that rolled out of his grandfather's mouth.

Angelo was enthralled with Piero's stories of personal courage and ideas about Italian liberty. He was, in fact, Piero's only audience. Soon he could not separate his grandfather's adventures and national pride from his own young life.

Angelo removed the last of the splinters. He put on his shoes and continued walking down the dock.

⚮ *two* ⚮

Piero took every opportunity to remind Angelo of the day of his birth, among other things. The significance of Piero's account of his grandson's squalling entry into the world was not lost on Angelo. On that very day, September 24, 1870, and for the first time in anyone's memory, Italy became a unified nation free of the foreign powers that had dominated her life for centuries.

Every time Angelo heard Piero's account of that simultaneous event—his birth and Italy's rebirth—he understood his grandfather a little better. Piero described that day so often and so vividly that Angelo clearly imagined the whole affair. It gave him an eerie sensation. It was as if he himself was a witness to his own coming, which of course he was, but not in the way Piero impressed the whole scene on his young, lively mind.

Once Piero triggered the double happening in his grandson's head, it became an unquestionable reality to Angelo.

He could see the thick mass of chanting Neopolitans standing in the noon heat of the Piazza Carita. He passed through the *piazza* or near it on his frequent trips to and from the dock. He could hear the steady chorus of "Roma! Roma! Roma!" beating a husky tattoo on the heavy air that lay low over the city like a wet blanket.

Angelo reached the street, thinking once again of what it was like the day he was born. He glanced at awesome Vesuvius, that ancient volcanic messenger of death and destruction. It stood off in the heat-hazy distance quietly expelling the smoky reminder of its fiery power. Overhead, a couple of hungry seagulls, up from the port district, wheeled about in sluggish expectation and curiosity.

Angelo lost himself in the noisy crowd. And the beat went on in his head just as Piero used to describe it, "Roma! Roma! Roma!"

At precisely five minutes past noon—as Angelo was told to remember it—the south rampart cannons of Castel San Elmo, high in the hills overlooking the throbbing, waiting crowd, fired a majestic salvo that split the hot, sodden air and shook the steamy, squalid and tilted streets of impoverished Naples below.

The cannons of Castel San Elmo were quiet today, however, as Angelo worked his way through the jostling throng. The streets of Naples were as steamy, squalid and tilted as they ever were.

Angelo's homeward shuffle turned into a steady gait as he turned in the direction of Piazza Carita. Now the beat in his head quickened. The chant changed. "Italia! Italia! Italia!" the crowd of twelve years ago screamed as it burst from the piazza and poured into the surrounding streets.

"*Libero! Libero! Libero!*"

"Free! Free! Free!"

Angelo no longer heard the noisy confusion of the streets. He heard the voice of his dead grandfather drowned by the cries of national passion leaping from the hoarse throat of the lurching mob and rolling across old Naples in a storm of sound. It was a moment of common joy that energized the Piazza Carita and environs, turning nearly every Neapolitan alley, avenue and square into spasms of unrestrained dancing, singing and merrymaking, engulfing all of Italy at the same time.

≫ *three* ≪

On one hot September day in 1870, centuries of national dismemberment, frustration and fighting had come to an end. The Italian national spirit had prevailed. Italy was whole. Italy was unified. And the people bellowed their satisfaction from one end of the land to the other. *Risorgimento*, the fifty-five-year period that witnessed the resurgence of Italian nationalism, was complete. Rome had fallen to an Italian army without bloodshed.

Rome, last of the city-states, had given in. Rome, last of the papal states—those great tracts of Italian territory ruled by generations of Popes, spiritual leaders of the Roman Catholic Church—had been ceded to the Kingdom of Italy.

(33)

Emperor Napoleon III, whose French troops had protected papal Rome, led his army in the final hours of a bitter war with Prussia. In a matter of four days—September 1 to September 4—he was defeated, captured at Sedan and deposed in Paris. France, humiliated, unable to maintain her presence anywhere, withdrew her troops from Rome.

Italian forces marched into the naked city. There they confined Pope Pius IX to the walled estates behind the huge baroque cathedral of Saint Peter and then handed over the rest of Rome to King Victor Emmanuel II.

The Pope angrily denounced the seizure and proclaimed himself a prisoner. It would take another sixty years to decide whether he was indeed a prisoner. In the end, Vatican City, home of the Holy Father and seat of the worldwide Roman Catholic Church, would become a state within a state, sovereign and independent, having a civil government of its own ruled over by the Pope, not the King of Italy. Other than a few particular churches scattered around Rome, there would be no other papal territory in Italy subject to the civil rule of the Pope.

Angelo never showed much enthusiasm for the history lessons that Piero offered. Piero knew a good deal less history than he was prepared to admit. What history he did know, however, were those events that he himself had participated in as a soldier, policeman and reveler. What always seemed to interest Angelo most of all were those cannons high up in the hills. He ached for the sound of them. He would give his precious shoes just to hear one earsplitting salvo. Instead—at least at the moment—all he seemed to hear was that long-ago mob roaring in their frenzied rhythm:

Rome! Rome! Rome!
Italy! Italy! Italy!
Free! Free! Free!

Not since the barbarians sacked Rome 1,460 years before Angelo

(35)

was born and destroyed the foundation of the Roman Empire had Italy been a self-governing, united country. Until the day of his birth, Italy the nation, Italy unified, was a myth and a dream that existed only in the minds of patriots like Piero Capello. The truth of the matter was that during those many centuries Italy was just a spiny peninsula with a brilliant past. She poked into the Mediterranean Sea like an ancient leg in a high-heeled boot upon which sat the body of Europe.

At one time or another, the Italian mainland was declared open season for everyone but Italians. A long succession of Austrians, Frenchmen, Spaniards, Holy Roman Emperors and ambitious Popes carved up Italy to suit their purposes. As far back as the 1500s, Swiss and German mercenaries roamed the land making it their special preserve of violence for anyone who could pay their price.

Between the convulsions of the French Revolution toward the end of the 1700s and the passing of Napoleon Bonaparte in 1815—about a quarter of a century—foreign domination of Italy was an overwhelming fact of life. Italians seemed to have no future. Italian destiny lay dormant, asleep in its miraculous art and architecture of centuries past. At stake were the exercises of power and the territorial aims of Austria, France and the Church.

Young Angelo Capello was aware of the national tragedy that had infected his country for so long—the tragedy of subjugation and the inability of the Italian people to unify and kick the foreign tyrants out. The country was on the brink of oblivion until his grandfather Piero rescued it—or so it seemed at times. Angelo did not know all of the historical details. He was not yet alive to experience the turmoil that Piero described. But Piero was a persistent teacher about his own spirit. And in the end it was a spirit of adventure that Piero passed on to Angelo, not the lingering nationalism of his fiery, romantic youth.

Angelo pushed through the crowd that seemed to shriek even louder as he neared Piazza Carita. The chanting, dancing Neapolitans that he continued to imagine knew more about what Piero felt than he did. It was their Naples that was wrenched from France by that popular hero-soldier, Giuseppe Garibaldi, ten years before he, Angelo Capello, was born. After that only Rome remained to be fused to the Italian body.

❧ *four* ❧

Angelo reached the sagging tenement on Vico Gallupi that the Capellos called home. The narrow brick house was not very ancient, as most things seemed to be in old Naples. Maybe twenty-four or twenty-five years at the most. It was five stories high and looked shabby enough to have been there a hundred years, at least. The bricks had been painted a dull yellow when the building was new. In the passing years much of the paint had peeled, revealing patches of splotchy red. The wood trim had once been painted a bright green. Now it was faded in the few spots that remained. The rest of the paint had long since peeled, too.

What really made the house look tired was the fact that it was not plumb. It was not exactly vertical. Squeezed between two wider, slightly taller apartment houses, it leaned against one of them. If it were not for the presence and the support of the more massive structure, the narrow, listing house would have fallen into a brick rubble—or so it seemed.

Nevertheless, there it was, upright. Once it belonged to Piero. Now it belonged to Angelo's grandmother, Louisa. The house had originally been given to Piero Capello by General Garibaldi himself for "services rendered"—for Piero's part in chasing the French out of Naples—and for the sergeant's pay he never received. When Piero

died, the house passed on to Louisa. By agreement, Louisa Capello could not bequeath the house to anyone. She would be the last owner.

There were tenants on the three top floors. The Capellos lived on the two bottom floors. Nobody paid any rent. And the Capellos paid no taxes—another reward for helping to restore Naples to Italy. Piero had kept his family alive on a small, policeman's wage. Luigi, his son, made small contributions first as a dockworker, then as a street fixer.

Angelo stood for a minute or two in front of the house and wondered whether he had arrived too early. Too early for what? He had no idea. It did not matter anyway. Maybe Vito, his younger brother, was somewhere around. They might find something to do together. The house seemed so quiet. There wasn't much traffic on the street either.

Angelo sat down in the shade of the front door and removed his shoes. He stretched his legs and wiggled his toes. The door opened behind him. Madelena appeared and surveyed her oldest son.

"What are you doing out there, Angelo?"

"Nothing."

"Then I have something for you to do. Come inside and clean yourself. Make yourself ready for tonight's celebration."

"What celebration?"

"What celebration! Your birthday! You are twelve years old today. Or have you forgotten?"

"No. I have not forgotten."

"Then come, Angelo. Your aunts and I have been busy with preparations all day. Can't you smell it? Mmmmmmm. Tonight we dine under the stars in the grape arbor in your honor."

"Without grandfather again."

"Without your grandfather."

Madelena disappeared into the coolness of the house. Angelo remained on the doorstep looking up and down the street as if he expected a great crush of people to come marching out of nowhere, led by Piero.

"That must have been something to see," Angelo told himself half aloud. Again Piero welled up in his mind as Angelo continued to remember his grandfather and the day of his own birth—Italy's too.

Wild-eyed and near hysteria, Piero had willingly welded himself to the crushing swarm of humanity that swept into the Via Simonelli, only a few yards from where Angelo now sat and brooded.

Forty years old then, rugged, bearded and a head taller than anyone around him, the darkly impressive Piero Capello had waited half a lifetime for that day. And to be washed up and down those sweaty streets by that passionate tide of Neapolitans on such an occasion was sheer ecstasy. Piero Capello, born in Naples and a lifelong tested patriot, was having the time of his life.

At eighteen, filled with dreams of Italian glory—or, perhaps just plain personal glory—and propelled by an empty stomach, Piero had gone north to join the forces of General Giuseppe Garibaldi, who was trying to rid Italy of the Austrians. He failed. Beaten at Custozza and Novara but not altogether crushed, Garibaldi turned south to attack the French garrison in Rome. Piero followed his general to Rome and fought well, but the French drove them off. On the outskirts of Rome, Piero found pretty Louisa Paoli, married her and retreated across the mountains with what was left of Garibaldi's army. That was in 1849.

A year later, Piero and Louisa were in Castellammare di Stabia, a little town on the southern rim of the Bay of Naples. Piero, now a known revolutionary with a price on his head—a French price—would not dare enter the French-ruled Kingdom of Naples. Here, in Castellammare, Angelo's father Luigi was born. And then came his aunts Rosa and Angelina; and his uncles Pasquale and Lorenzo. None of the children were named after Piero's hero, General Garibaldi. Louisa would not hear of it. It was one way she had devised of putting an end to her husband's battle-scarred past and his life as a soldier.

(40)

As for Piero, unskilled at everything but the soldier's trade, he spent his days dreaming of plots against the French, going to secret meetings and otherwise listlessly working around the little shipyards of Castellammare, scratching out a meager living. He became a bit poorer each year and more bitter. Still the fires of hope and revolution burned within him.

Late one sultry August afternoon, ten years after arriving in Castellammare, Piero burst into the family hovel.

Angelo knew this part of his grandfather's life as he knew the back of his hand. It was as real in his mind as if he himself had been there to see and listen to all that went on.

"Garibaldi is back!" Piero screamed.

"Where? I can't see him," Louisa retorted in a mocking tone.

"Sicily!" Piero shouted. "Sicily! He has taken Sicily!"

"Piero, my husband, we are seven mouths. Can your brave general put bread in them? We are here. He is there. The sea and starvation still separate us."

"Ah, Louisa, we shall settle that."

"How? Become a soldier again? And this time go to your early grave? You have children to think about. Do you want to leave them alone? Hungry? No papa? For what? A dream? Be a farmer instead and let us eat."

"Sssh. Louisa, listen to me. There is no work here. There is no work anywhere. Not for me. Not for any son of Italy. Unless, of course, one shines the boots of the foreigners. I cannot do that. I cannot even go to Naples where I belong. There are too many dead Frenchmen in my past. I am not a farmer. I am a soldier. I know how to fight. I have been there before. Garibaldi needs the likes of me. Now! And we need Italy free. Now! When Italy belongs to us, then there will be work for everyone. There will be food for all. Then and only then will I never have to soldier again. But in the meantime I shall fight. My children will know what their papa did. And some day my grandchildren will know. And they will all be proud."

"Bah!" Louisa muttered.

"Since you say, Louisa, that Garibaldi is there and we are here; and that the sea and starvation are in between, we shall cross the sea, join the army and eat.

"Right, Luigi?" Piero asked his eldest son.

"Right, Papa." Luigi threw his father a crisp salute. Piero roared with delight.

"There! You see. Ten years old and already he knows what has to be done. We are going to march with Garibaldi again. We shall have Naples and we shall not stop until the Pope himself hands over Rome."

With this last outburst, Piero crossed himself. Louisa fled to a small, nearby church where she appealed to the Virgin Mary to forgive her husband for what he said about the Pope.

The next day, irrepressible Piero Capello packed himself, Louisa and their five children aboard a sleazy coastal trader and sailed for Sicily.

Two days later, having been somewhat delayed by a cranky steam boiler and little wind to fill a tattered sail, the Capellos wearily stepped ashore at Messina.

Two days more after that, Piero—Sergeant Piero Capello—was once again a soldier in General Giuseppe Garibaldi's thousand-man Red Shirt Army, poised for an attack on Naples.

⊰ *five* ⊱

Luigi came trudging up the street bent under the burden of a couple of shovels and a pick. He straightened up a bit when he spied Angelo sitting on the doorstep staring vacantly into space.

"Angelo, my son, why do you look so unhappy? Today is your birthday. You are twelve years old today. You are now a wise and ancient fellow. You should be smiling at your luck, not frowning."

Luigi put down his tools and sat down next to his son. "What troubles you?" he asked. "Are we not to have a feast in your honor tonight?"

"Yes, Papa. There will be a feast. Mama has already told me to get cleaned up."

"Well, you look clean enough to me—except for your feet. It must be something else—something important."

"Grandfather," Angelo answered in a single word.

"Ah. Yes. I might have known it. You miss him. We all miss him. But I do not think that your grandfather who looks down on you this very minute from Heaven would want you to be so sad on a day that was the most important day in his life."

"You don't think so, Papa?"

"I am sure of what I say, Angelo. I tell you, my son, Piero Capello—God rest his soul—is smiling right now. Did I ever tell you what he did while you were being born?"

Angelo was certain of the story that was to come but he had no chance to stop his own father from reaching into his memory. Luigi was not about to give Angelo the opportunity of saying that he had heard it before. Luigi continued without taking a breath.

"Papa stumbled out of the crowd that filled this street and fell right through this door—this very door—into the front room. Your mother was in the next room. I was sitting in the corner chair stiff as a board worrying about your mama—the same chair in the same corner that hasn't been moved in twelve years.

"When papa saw me he wanted to know if I had turned to stone.

" 'Be proud,' he said to me. 'Italy has become a country. Soon we shall have an empire again. Today, Luigi,' he told me, 'you shall give Italy a son.'

(43)

"That was just like papa," Luigi went on. "First came Italy, then came his grandchild.

"Do you know what I said to papa? I said, 'Not me, Papa. Madelena will give Italy a son.'

"And then mama asked papa what he would do if you were a girl instead of a boy. Of course you turned out to be a boy, but no one knew then what you would be. Only papa. He knew.

"You should have seen him, Angelo. What a sight he was!"

Luigi went on to describe in some detail how Piero straightened himself to his full height, stuck out his jaw and put his hands behind his back as he glared angrily at his wife, Louisa. His red "Garibaldi" army shirt was half out of his soiled, white pants. The red, white and green sash of his veterans' club was twisted around his torso in such disarray that his five medals—one each for the Battles of Custozza, Novara, Rome and Naples, and one for special bravery at Rome—were tangled together on his right hip rather than on his chest. Somewhere in the joyous crowd he had lost his black, tasseled campaign cap. His breath was thick with wine.

Angelo had never heard this part of his grandfather's story before. Piero had never mentioned his disheveled appearance except to say that he had lost his cap in the crowd. And he never mentioned Louisa's annoyance with him. Luigi fell silent, momentarily soaking up the memory of Angelo's birth as if it had happened yesterday instead of twelve years ago.

Angelo pleaded for more. "Go on, Papa. What was it that grandfather did?"

"Well," Luigi continued, "and mind you, the front door was still open. No one had bothered to shut it after papa had fallen into the house. A few strangers were standing there listening to mama make a speech.

" 'Look at you,' she said to papa. 'My hero!' she called him. 'Con-

(44)

queror of Naples! Hail, Caesar!' I remember her saying. 'What a palace you have given us! What riches you have spread at our feet! What feasts we have known! And are we or Italy any better off today than we were yesterday or will be tomorrow! Here sits your son, Luigi, frightened for his Madelena; worried for his future; while you, a poor man, speak of an empire.' "

Again Madelena came to the door. This time she came to see what was keeping Angelo.

"Ah. Luigi. You are home early. Have you seen Vito anywhere? He should have been home an hour ago. Are you two coming inside?"

"In a minute, Mama. Papa and I are discussing important matters."

"Yes. Give us another minute, Madelena. We shall be right along."

Luigi turned to Angelo as the door behind them softly closed. He took up his account once more.

"Funny thing, Angelo, I clearly remember hearing a band of military musicians quick-marching past the front door, blasting the air with martial music just as your grandmother finished her speech. Anyway, papa marched over to me very straight. He had put his shirt in his pants and fixed the sash so that all his medals hung correctly."

"And then what happened, Papa?" Angelo had never heard any of this either. His excitement was rising as he sensed a climax was near.

"Papa pointed to his medal for bravery at Rome," Luigi continued, "and asked me to look at this honor. I looked. It took my mind off things. I had seen it a thousand times before. Then he said he had not won it for bravery at the gates of Rome. You can imagine my surprise. No, said papa, he had won it at the Battle of Louisa Paoli.

"It was a joke, Angelo. And we both laughed. That was good. Then I stood up and gave papa a snappy salute just like I used to do when I was about your age. Suddenly papa started to cry and I started to cry and you, Angelo, you cried. What a moment that was! Mama and your aunts Rosa and Angelina rushed into the room and announced that I had a son. Believe it or not, Angelo, right then and

(45)

there the strangers in the doorway applauded. We had all forgotten about them. And that military band came by again. The whole thing sounded like a chorus of angels to me.

"And then it happened. Your grandmother shut the door. And papa made a speech. No one could stop him. And I remember every word of it because of what he did when he finished.

" 'You have made us proud today, Luigi,' papa said. 'We have much to celebrate. The birth of a new generation of Capellos and the birth of Italy.'

"This time, Angelo, your grandfather put us ahead of Italy.

" 'We are joined with history,' papa went on. 'Forever! You are a good son, Luigi. You will be a brave father. I cannot always say the same for myself. In some ways I am a very rich man. It is so because I have lived to be a happy witness to all this. In most ways I am a very poor man. My pockets are empty. And this house is worthless to my children. Those were the terms. But I want you, Luigi, to have something of mine to remember this day.'

"Papa then took off his medal for bravery at Rome and pinned it on my shirt. 'Long live Italy!' he shouted. 'Long live the Capellos!' And that was that.

"Some day, Angelo," Luigi told his son, "that medal will be yours. But you have to earn it. Do you think you are ready to begin?"

"Yes, Papa. I am ready," Angelo responded with his first smile of the day.

"Good. I hear your mama calling. It is time for celebration."

≈ six ≈

Peace and quiet had come to the sagging house on the Vico Galluppi. Angelo's birthday feast was a cheerful, boisterous success. The backyard had been full with Capellos and La Starzas—Madelena's family—and a few neighbors, including the upstairs tenants. Everyone had worn themselves out eating and drinking on a day that few would recall in detail in years to come. The La Starzas and others had gone home. Only those who lived in the Capello house remained to dwell on the happy events of the evening, capped by a great feast under the Neapolitan sky.

The rest of Naples was at home, too, exhausted, having taken hours to eat its way through the customary evening meal. By midnight, the city was still. Here and there a few couples promenaded along the waterfront, their forms silhouetted against the smooth waters of the bay, twinkling beneath a high moon.

Angelo lay awake in his bed staring into the dark corners of his room. A few feet away lay his brothers and sisters—fast asleep. His mind was alive with wonder about what he must do to earn his grandfather's medal for bravery now that he was twelve years old. He fell asleep seeing himself as a great warrior-hero conquering a distant land.

Luigi, too, lay awake in his bed next to the sleeping Madelena thinking of his earlier conversation with Angelo and what meaning his father's medal for bravery held for him. As he too stared into dark corners, pondering the future in Naples, the soft timbre of his father's voice seemed to drift into the room from somewhere out near the grape arbor where everyone had celebrated Angelo's birthday and caressed him with loving music. Luigi, dreaming his own uncertain dreams, fell asleep to the distant strains of a melodic air that described the incomparable Neapolitan sunshine and peace following a storm—"O Sole Mio."

Che bella cosa 'na iurnata 'e sole
N' aria serena doppo 'na tempesta!
Pe'll' aria fresca pare già na' festa,
Che bella cosa 'na iurnata 'e sole.

Ma n'atu sole
Cchiù bello, oi ne',
O sole mio
Sta 'nfronte a te!
O sole, o sole mio
Sta 'nfronte a te!

III

Addio

April 18, 1883

Wednesday

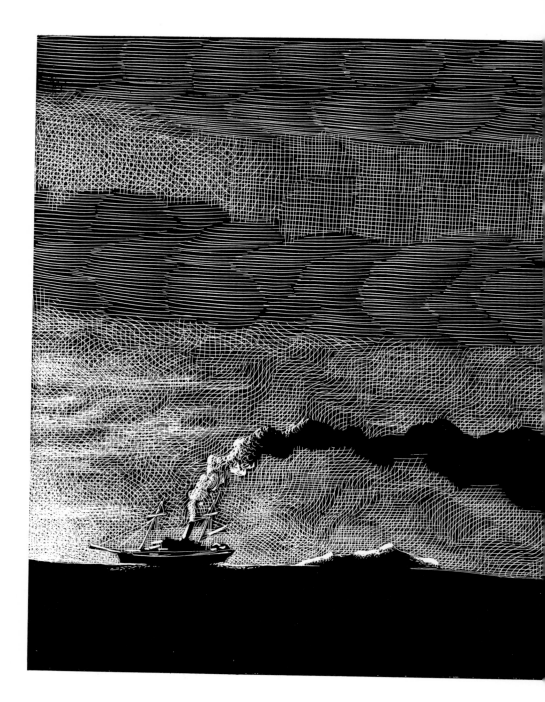

⪺ *one* ⪻

Angelo Capello was something special to his grandfather, Piero Capello, the poor, dreamy policeman without ambition. Angelo was
something beyond the extension of Piero's warm Neapolitan blood-
line. Angelo was not just a boy. Angelo was not just a first grandchild,
a first grandson. Nor was it that he was the first son of Madelena and
Luigi Capello. In his grandfather's mind, Angelo Capello was Italy
reincarnate. Born on the very day that Italy rose from her manacled
sleep of centuries and stood as a nation among nations, Angelo Capello
was the living symbol of his grandfather's idealism.

Angelo's grandmother, Louisa, became more cranky and impatient
with her husband, Piero, as he happily regaled his young grandson
with glorious Garibaldi stories. She chided him for his unwillingness
to see things as they had been, as they are and as they probably will
go on being. Louisa, the tired, family workhorse, could never accept
their poverty for the greater good of the Italian State.

"Leave Angelo be, Piero," she pleaded time and again. "Stop filling
his head with useless dreams and fairy tales. Look at your own sons!
Ditchdiggers! And no thanks to you! And what of your daughters?
Unwed flowers! Condemned to die hanging out the wash over the
filthy streets of sunny Naples. Where are all the opportunities you
promised?"

"Enough!" Piero would scream.

The battles between Louisa and Piero grew fiercer with the arrival
of each new grandchild.

Now there were Vito, Teresa, Fausto, Tomasina, Maria and
Giovanni. Only Angelo fired his grandfather's spirit. He was the
first. None of the others enjoyed the distinction of having been born
on Italy's own modern birthday.

Angelo was six years old when the last of the children was born—

Giovanni. His brother's arrival made little impact on Angelo. He un-
_____ little of what was going on inside the constant cyclone of
no. _____ rled about him, either in the house or on the streets. Not
even _____ dfather made sense all the time. His mother, Madelena,
had grown at and weary. But Angelo could not have known the
beautiful slip of a girl his father had married. Luigi himself at times
looked older than his own father, worn out by responsibilities and
backbreaking labors on the cobbled streets.

"Have courage" was all that Piero could tell his eldest son.

Louisa and her daughters, Rosa and Angelina, had become as thin as
sticks. Her two younger sons, Pasquale and Lorenzo, had gone north
in search of their futures.

The poor of Naples, already packed into the steamy, congested
streets that ringed the blue bay like an amphitheater, were jammed
deeper into their sunny misery by their own countrymen. Southern
farmers from Calabria and Sicily, desperate, unable to make their tired
land yield decent crops, came north in search of *their* futures. Some
of them found it—on ships bound for America. Many more would follow. Soon the trickle of immigrants would become a raging stampede
of outbound Italians. Naples would roar with the sound of their des-
peration and departure.

Meanwhile, Louisa Capello continued her personal storming of her
undaunted Piero.

"What are we?" Louisa would ask remorselessly. And then she
would answer her own question. "Nothing."

Before Piero had a chance to draw a breath in his continuing de-
fense, Louisa would be at him again. "Did Garibaldi make of you
something you could not have made yourself? He does not even remember you."

"I am a policeman. I have respect. I am a veteran. I have honor,"
Piero always answered.

"Policeman!" Louisa shrieked. "Respect! Honor! What do you

(55)

police? The back door of the San Carlo Opera House! The fish market! The docks! The cafés! And for what? What do they pay you, Signor Policeman? *Fagioli!* Beans!"

Louisa would spit the word out with utter contempt. *Fagioli.*

More than once she reminded Piero that he did not fight to become a slave in the House of Savoy—Italy's ruling family. "What happened to your pride?"

Piero would hold his head high and answer, "We have Victor Emmanuel II, an Italian, for a King. We do not have a Frenchman, nor an Austrian, nor a Pope for a King. That is my pride."

"And are we better off now, because we have Victor Emmanuel—better off now than we were before you helped put him on his throne?"

"Yes! Yes! Yes!" Piero never failed to exclaim.

"No! No! No!" Louisa never failed to answer. And she would flee the house to seek the peace and quiet of San Liborio. There she would light a candle in a small, dark chapel and pray for the salvation of all the Capellos.

Piero, usually stranded by the bitter quiet following these outbursts, sought *his* peace and solace in his grandson Angelo. They took long walks together, sometimes in the back hills, sometimes along the waterfront. Angelo preferred the waterfront, where he could keep his eye on the horizon and the mysteries that lay beyond.

Angelo sensed his grandmother's disappointments. All he had to do was look at the deeply etched lines that crisscrossed the sad and sunburnt face of his father, Luigi. His grandfather did not seem to have such lines on his face. Not even Piero's bushy beard could hide lines like that. Angelo seemed to understand Piero, too. At least he understood the pride and hope that drove him into a Neapolitan world of his own.

"Your grandfather thinks he is the soul of Italy," Luigi told Angelo one quiet evening under the grape arbor.

"But he *is* the soul of Italy, Papa."

"What makes you think so, Angelo?"

"He told me so himself."

"And you believe him?"

"Yes, I believe him."

"Why?" asked the persistent Luigi.

"Because, Papa, in his own happiness, in his own dreams, he suffers. And Italy, in its own happiness, in its own dreams, suffers still."

Luigi Capello was stunned by the perception of his young son.

"These things take time, Angelo. The King is smart. He and his clever ministers are making great plans for all of us."

"That's what grandpa always says, Papa. But how much time?"

Luigi had no answer to Angelo's question. What did he, Luigi, know anyway? He was not educated. He was not clever. He was only a fixer of streets with seven children and a wife.

"Soon, Angelo, very soon," he replied, while thinking to himself, "Never."

In that quick exchange, Luigi Capello saw the future and was frozen with apprehension. He stared at his son in the gloom of the arbor. He considered the rest of the children. Unlike Piero, the idealist, Luigi the realist saw all of his children destined to live meager lives, fix streets, learn nothing and earn beans.

A flash of anger swept over him as he suddenly envisioned a monstrous betrayal of his father's ancient victories, leaving them all with no real opportunities for a better life. It never occurred to Luigi to pin some of the blame on his own father, whose idea for national and family improvement was to chase the French out of Naples—an heroic event that occurred a generation ago.

Naples may be the juice of life for his father, thought Luigi, but for his mother it has been a bitter cup. He himself could endure his lowly station. Madelena would endure it with him. But not his children! They deserved a chance—a better life. How proud this would make him if he, Luigi Capello, could make it possible. The answer lay somewhere outside of Naples.

Right then and there, in those electrifying minutes, Luigi Capello resolved to devote his life to that end. Like Moses and the Israelites, he, Luigi Capello, would lead his tribe out of the land of their servitude to a more promising place.

"Angelo," Madelena called. "Is that you out there with your father?"

"Yes, Mama."

"It's time for bed."

≫ *two* ≪

Luigi Capello awoke each dawn with more purpose than he ever expected to have. He went to work with a freshness of spirit that first puzzled Madelena, then worried her.

"Do you feel well, Luigi?"

"I am fine."

"Are you unhappy?"

"Do I look unhappy? Do I say unhappy things? Do I act unhappy?"

"No."

"Then why do you ask such foolish questions?"

Something was in the wind. Madelena knew it. Luigi was different. And whatever it was, he was not talking about it. The more he kept his silence, the more Madelena convinced herself that Luigi was planning a monstrous crime. Angelo saw no particular change in his father except, perhaps, that he appeared a bit more buoyant—almost cheerful. Other than that, Angelo suspected nothing. Neither did anyone else.

Madelena, afraid to ask any questions, simply told Luigi to be careful. And this she did without fail every time Luigi left the house.

Luigi kept his idea to himself. He was not ready to discuss the matter with anyone. He knew that if he as much as hinted or joked about leaving Naples, Madelena would complain and howl, although in the end she would understand and go along. His father, Piero, on the other hand, would never understand. He would probably rage against any move that would remove his grandchildren from his sight, particularly Angelo. His mother, Louisa, might very well approve, but not without plenty of tears. As for Madelena's own family, her parents and brothers, Luigi doubted if they would accept any decision he made, good or bad, right or wrong, about anything.

For the moment, Luigi would have to keep his own counsel. All he had was an idea. There was no form to it, no shape, no direction. Actually, whether Luigi realized it or not, he did make one firm decision—to get out of Naples and try his luck elsewhere—just where was something else again. And until he knew where and how to get there, he would remain silent.

◈ *three* ◈

The harbor noise was constant and shrill. It did not even subside at noon when most Neapolitans usually quit the high sun, their labors and shops to eat and nap in their own homes. It was a national habit to work all morning, take a long midday break and then return to work during the late afternoon for several more hours. But not today. The national habit was temporarily suspended. No one seemed to want to go home. The port was clogged with ships and crowded with people.

A steady stream of travelers lugging bundles, meager belongings and children—always children, children everywhere—tramped up the groaning gangplanks of the gently heaving ships. Most of them were young—in their twenties. If there were any old people among them, they were hardly noticeable. Many of these emigrants—in fact, the overwhelming majority of them—were southern farmers, short, wiry, dark-complected men and women who did not look back once they set foot on the gangplanks. Caught between an unproductive past, interminable poverty and a foreign future, they would not look back. They could not look back.

Descendants of the ancient Greeks who first colonized southern Italy, descendants of the early Romans, Saracens and Carthaginians, they would never escape their deeply rooted, vital past, joined for so many centuries to the soil of Italy. The past would be with them always. Now all they had was the uncertain future, their children and a few bundles. They did not smile. They did not cry. They looked straight ahead.

On this particular September day of 1881, there were only several hundred seeking new lives outside of Italy. In twenty years there would be at least a million Italians—chiefly from Sicily, Naples and everywhere south of Naples—reaching for new lives beyond the Italian peninsula.

Swarms of Italians intermingled around the gangplanks, on the dockside streets and wherever a dozen or more of their departing countrymen would appear to begin their voyage. There were clusters of Neapolitans looking on the scene with fascination. They had witnessed from time to time the departure of hopeful people, but they had never seen so many leaving at one time. Street vendors hawked their wares and did a brisk business among the departing farmers—pots and pans to take along; food for the long voyage; clothing; combs; buttons and miscellaneous sundries like needle and thread that one might need in a strange land.

Piero Capello, on duty and accompanied by Angelo, moved through

the throng with an imperious air that suggested the authority of an emperor. With his hands behind his back and his head held high, he looked down from his nearly six-foot frame upon the shuffling emigrants.

Angelo walked a few steps behind his grandfather, twisting this way and turning that way, trying to take in every sight and sound at once. Every so often Piero would look back to see if Angelo was still there, with him, and not aimlessly wandering off.

Luigi, fixing a street at the edge of the crowd, caught a glimpse of his father and son. He shook his head at his father's pompous impression, wished Angelo would find better things to do and went on digging up the street while surveying the ships and people. He thought some more about leaving Naples.

Piero was plainly distressed as he and Angelo mixed with the crowd.

"Did you ever see such a thing before, Angelo?"

"What thing, Grandfather?"

"All these people. All these ships."

"No. Where are they going?"

"Away, Angelo. Away. Away from Italy. Forever. Look at them, my grandson. Look how young and strong they are. Italy needs them now. And they leave."

"Hey! Hey, you. Over there! Yes. You. You with the baby."

A young couple with an infant stepped out of a knot of people, singled out for some unexplained reason by a policeman. Fear clouded their faces—and those around them—as Piero approached.

"What is wrong, sir? Have we done anything wrong?"

The couple was worried. They were on their way to begin new lives in a distant place. A strutting Italian policeman was the last person in the world they wanted anything to do with. He might stop them from boarding their ship for some ridiculous reason. They wanted no part of Piero Capello. But there was little they could do about it.

"What have we done, sir?"

"Nothing. Nothing at all. Be calm everyone," Piero intoned, sweeping his arms over the cluster of people as if he were bestowing a priestly—no, papal—blessing. "I have a few questions. Nothing official, mind you. Some questions to satisfy the curiosity of this small boy here," he said pointing to Angelo.

Angelo looked startled. He did not put his grandfather up to this impromptu interrogation. Angelo shrugged, guessing correctly that Piero was about to give him a lesson in loyalty to Italy at the expense of these people.

"First. Would you tell me your name and where you are from?"

"Yes," answered the young man, his face visibly relaxing. "I am Mario Scarpellino. This is my wife Sabina. And this is our daughter, Marta. All the others you see here are my brothers, my sisters and my cousins. We are all from Moliterno. It is far to the south of here. Have you heard of Moliterno?"

"Ah ha," Piero softly grunted, indicating that he had heard of Moliterno, which of course he had not. "Where are you going?"

"We are going to America. Sabina, Marta and I."

"And the others?" asked Piero, gesturing around. "Pay attention Angelo, you will learn something."

"They will come someday, too," the young man replied sadly, looking from one relative to the next. "But I see," he went on looking directly at Piero, "that you, Mr. Policeman, have to have the whole story. So, I shall tell you.

"It's a very simple story. We are poor and humble people—not stupid, mind you—just poor and humble. There are many like us in Moliterno. Until a year or two ago—maybe three—we worked a pitiful piece of land and managed to grow enough to keep us and our oxen from starving to death. We were never far from that—starving to death. We lived and died on that land from the time Christ was a baby."

(64)

Sabina, his wife, crossed herself. Piero wasn't sure he wanted the account to continue.

"Suddenly, the land gave up. It was too old. It was too dry. It grew nothing. We were destined for early graves. It was decided by my papa and my uncles that we, the young ones, should go north to find work, new lives and perhaps send money and food back to the old ones. We came as far north as Naples. Here we found nothing but our misery. There was nothing for us in Naples. A few days ago I met a man from this ship—this ship, right here. He said I should go to America where there was work for everyone and everyone was rich. I told him I had no money for such a voyage. He said I did not need any. All that would be required would be my services for a few years. If I agreed to serve a certain man in the big city of New York in America, this *padrone*, this great man—a countryman, no less—would pay not only for my passage, but for Sabina's and Marta's as well.

"At first I refused. How could we leave the old ones and go so far? How could I leave my brothers, my sisters, my cousins and go so far? How could I leave Italy! I asked myself these questions many times over. And do you know what? I found that I could do it. That I could go. That Sabina could go. It is our destiny. There is no life here anymore for us.

"When the man gave me a paper to read and to sign, I was ashamed. I could neither read nor write. When I asked the man to take my brothers, my sisters and my cousins, he said that he would. Next year. And this he promised if I turned out to be a good worker. I put my mark on that paper. I shall be a good worker. I am happy to go. I shall be an American. I shall learn to read and to write. He promised me this too. I shall be a man, not a beggar."

Angelo listened intently as his grandfather shook his head from side to side.

"It is a sad story you tell, my young friend," Piero began. "I understand how you have been driven to do this—to leave your native land

and your loved ones. But Italy is new at being a country. Italy is only eleven years old. America is much older."

"That is not so, Mr. Policeman," Mario Scarpellino interrupted. "Italy is as old as the world is old. Moliterno, where I come from, is older than all of America."

"Where is your faith?" Piero went on, ignoring the interruption. "Where is your patience? You are young. I know it is for the young to do daring things as you are doing. I offer myself as a living example of that, for I too was young once and did daring things. But I did them for Italy as you should be doing. It is Italy that needs you, not America!

"I shall tell you something else, too. Do you think for one minute that this *padrone* of yours—this American *padrone*—is truly interested in your welfare? Or the welfare of your wife and baby? No! He will make a slave of you to fill his own pockets. He will use you for the rest of your life. You wi——"

"For five years," Mario insisted. "The paper said so!"

"How can you be sure? You said yourself you could not read. No, my young friend. You will be used until you die. And you will die poorer than you are now because you will be in his debt—a debt you cannot repay with simple hard labor. He will own you! He will own you because it will be the only way you shall have to give your family the riches you dream of. Without the *padrone* you will be torn to pieces by savages."

"If what you say is so, Mr. Policeman, then there is little difference between here and there. At least we shall eat, and that will make our chances better than they are now. We are without hope in Italy."

"I was a soldier of the Revolution," Piero solemnly responded. "The Revolution is your hope."

"Some Revolution!" Mario Scarpellino bitterly exclaimed. "Who remembers? Who cares? And who cares about us?"

With that, the young man turned his back on Piero and Angelo

Capello. With a show of defiance and measured determination, he jerked his wife and baby toward the gangplank, presented his documents to an official and marched up the wood ramp to meet the future.

Piero casually walked away. Angelo followed him. What a fool, Piero thought to himself. He'll probably get so seasick on that tub of a ship, he'll wish he'd never left the farm.

"Well, Angelo, what did you make of all that?"

"I don't know, Grandfather. I just don't know. There are a lot of people like that around here. There must be some truth to what he said. Everyone speaks of America as such a rich place. I have heard it before. They say that they have so much gold over there, that some streets are actually paved with it."

Piero burst out laughing. "And you believe that rot, Angelo?"

"Why not, Grandfather. Haven't you ever noticed how much happier American sailors seem to be than others? And how much bigger and stronger they are? And how much more money they always have than anyone else? Sometimes I think that I would like to see for myself what the truth is. If I ever do, Grandfather, I shall tell it to you first."

Piero detected a strong sign of rebellion in his grandson. He was not altogether sure that Angelo did not want to creep aboard one of these vessels and cross the sea to learn the truth, today. Piero began to walk a little faster.

"You know, Angelo, I know something about America. I read the daily paper. They are lunatics over there. Not long ago the American president was shot. He will probably die. His name is Garfield. The man who shot him wanted a job. They are lunatics, I tell you."

❧ *four* ❦

Luigi Capello leaned against his shovel and wistfully looked at the jumble of ships tied up along the crescent-shaped harbor.

"It's time to go home, Luigi," another workman observed. "We've labored hard enough for one morning. This is a thankless hole we've fixed. By this time next week the patch will be gone and the hole will be back. Have you any idea how many times it has been fixed? Five times in five weeks. And for what?"

"Beans," said Luigi half aloud.

"Eh?"

"Nothing. Never mind, Vittorio. Why don't you go home? I think I'll stay around awhile and watch the ships."

"Perhaps, Luigi, you are thinking of scrambling aboard one of them when no one is looking and sailing away to paradise like that bunch over there? I might be thinking the same thing if I had a wife and seven children."

Luigi glanced to his left and saw a half-dozen people with boxes and bundles heading toward the nearest ship. They were followed by a large mob of friends and relatives all dressed in their best holiday black. The entourage looked more like mourners than a bon-voyage committee.

"Perhaps, Vittorio. Perhaps."

Luigi continued to follow the procession hustling toward the ship as it crossed his line of vision. In one brief flash he saw himself, Madelena and the children, all carrying bundles and boxes and followed by everyone in both their families. Luigi's mental picture of their departure was so vivid he shuddered and snapped his head to bring himself back to reality.

Luigi Capello put down his shovel. He shook off his momentary hallucination once more and ambled toward the crowd. Just by chance, he thought, he might run into Angelo and his father—that is, if they were not already on their way home.

≽ *five* ≼

"Lunatics I tell you, Angelo. Lunatics."

Piero continued to lecture Angelo as they moved farther away from the docks in the direction of the Piazza del Mercato.

"Imagine shooting King Victor Emmanuel because he did not have work for you! Unthinkable! But that is exactly what happened to the American president. If the situation is so bad in America, what can our people expect to find there. Tell me! What can they expect?"

"I don't know, Grandfather. Do you really think it is that terrible?" Angelo wanted to know.

"Of course," Piero insisted with absolute conviction.

The news accounts, however, were not quite so black and white as Piero had interpreted them. The truth of the matter was that early in July a well-born man, Charles J. Guiteau, stepped up to the President of the United States in Union Station, Washington, and shot him twice. Guiteau did not need a job. What he wanted was a presidential appointment to some high public office. Disappointed that such a position would not be available to him, Guiteau, warped and deranged by his fury, resorted to assassination.

President Garfield clung to life for weeks before he finally died on September 19. Neither Piero Capello nor anyone else in Naples knew that the American president had died. His life had ended only yesterday. Few even knew or cared who the American president was. The average Neapolitan—the man on the street—had no keen interest in American affairs. Most of those now boarding the ships that would take them to America had no idea about American life, let alone

American politics and personalities. The death of an American president, in or out of office, was too distant an incident in the life of noisy Naples.

The only exception, perhaps, was Abraham Lincoln. Older Neapolitans were familiar with Lincoln's life and troubles. In some vague way they saw a connection—a parallel—between the American Civil War, that tore up that country at the same time the French were being run out of Naples, and their own battles; between the binding up of a dismembered America and the reunification of Italy; between the American issue of slavery and freedom and their own freedom after years of servitude as subjects of foreign rule.

The only connection Piero Capello could make between America and himself was a private one that surfaced every so often whenever he would idly review the trials and victories of his once-upon-a-time general, Giuseppe Garibaldi.

Some thirty years before, General Garibaldi had lived peacefully in America—on New York City's Staten Island. There he worked for a brief time as a candlemaker while revolution festered within him. Piero Capello knew all about his idol's American sojourn. But he never thought it important enough to dwell on. Luigi had heard about it once. Angelo had no idea about Garibaldi's American life at all. So far as Angelo was concerned, it was more important to hear about the battles. His grandfather, Piero, never failed him with those stories. It gave him a chance to relive glorious moments.

In recent weeks, especially today, with so many discontented Italians thinking and talking about leaving the country—and some of them desperate enough to do it—Garibaldi's American connection took on a slightly different cast in Piero Capello's mind. It was not that there was more meaning to what Piero thought about Garibaldi living on Staten Island. He seemed to remember it more. Just the thought of it invaded his thoughts with more regularity than before. There were other things about America and Garibaldi that Piero knew and never

(71)

mentioned. These he consigned to the most distant parts of his memories. But these too were now becoming part of his awareness.

Piero's Garibaldi remembrances flooded his mind as he and Angelo crossed a congested street and entered the public marketplace. Until a half-hour ago, this was the noisiest, tangiest smelling place in all Naples. Many of the vendors had already closed their shops and stalls. Some of them had gone home. Others preferred to mingle with the crowds at the docks. Here and there a few market people were washing down their small produce sections with buckets of water collected at the central fountain, a mediocre piece of sculpture. The fountain itself was a circular pond ringed by a knee-high concrete wall. Out of the pond leaped four scaly fish, frozen forever in their marbleized flight. Out of their mouths trickled an endless stream of lukewarm water. Each of the four fish faced in a different direction. Rising out of the center of the group was the great God of the Ocean Deep, Neptune—Neptune to the ancient Romans; Poseidon to the ancient Greeks.

The fountain was about two hundred years old. No one knew who designed it or who the sculptor was, except, perhaps, some scholar high up in the hills closeted in the University's Department of Antiquities. It did not matter anyway. No one paid the slightest attention to the fountain. To most Neapolitans it was a mechanical flop. To the very devout Catholic population it was a pagan abomination that should have died with the Roman Empire and the coming of Christianity. To Angelo and his grandfather it was a place to sit for a few minutes before continuing on their way.

Angelo splashed some of the warm water on his face and the back of his neck. Piero pulled a red handkerchief out of his trouser pocket, dipped it in the water and tied the soaking cloth around his neck. The two of them sat silently on the low wall and surveyed the near empty marketplace baking under the noon sun. Presently the two of them moved off.

As they reached the corner of an alley that would lead them out of the area, an old lady swilled a bucket of water down the narrow, dank passageway. The alley was alive with garbage and the sweet aroma of rotting cabbage leaves. The old lady was doing the best she could to rid the alley of both the sweet stink and the leavings. All she succeeded in doing on her first try was to make the going as slippery as a cake of fresh ice. She disappeared behind a wall to refill her bucket as Angelo and Piero rounded the corner.

"Look out, Grandfather!"

The warning was instantaneous and too late.

Angelo skidded some two or three feet before falling on the slime. Piero, right behind him, literally flew through the air feet first. He fell heavily, soundlessly, the back of his head slamming onto the slick stones before the rest of him hit the ground.

Angelo got up slowly. Piero did not move. The old lady returned with a fresh bucket of water. Before she realized that anyone was in the alley she rinsed it again, drenching both Angelo and his unconscious grandfather. The dousing seemed to bring Piero around. His eyes flickered, opened and stared at the sky. Other than that, Piero did not move.

Stunned by the prostrate form of his grandfather, Angelo looked wildly about and then at the old woman. Terrified by the blinking but unmoving policeman on the stones and the look on Angelo's face, she fled indoors. Angelo tried to shout for help. The words would not come. He leaned alongside Piero and held his grandfather's limp, cold, wet hand. Tears swam around in his eyes and fell down his cheeks, mixing with the water still dripping from his soaked hair.

Finally, Angelo managed to ask Piero where he hurt.

"In the back of my head," Piero whispered. "I do not seem to be able to move either."

(73)

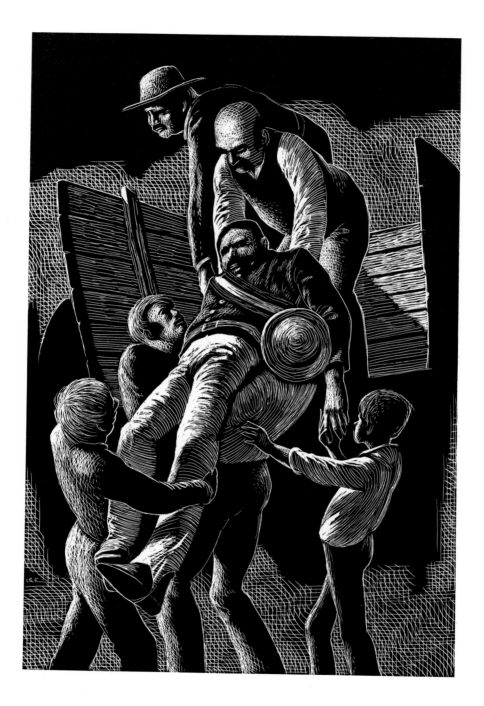

≫ *six* ≪

They brought Piero Capello home in a wagon.

Four or five people who had gathered at the scene of the accident gently lifted the policeman into the wagon hitched to a donkey. Only Angelo climbed into the wagon. A small crowd escorted the wagon to the drooping house on Vico Galluppi.

Piero was alert but paralyzed. He could see, hear and talk, but he was unable to move any part of himself. All the way home—a slow, plodding journey in a wagon pulled by a balky donkey and pushed by a determined collection of sympathetic people—Piero complained to Angelo that the only thing he could feel was a constant pain in his neck.

"Is that all, Grandfather?" said Angelo, trying to be cheerful. "In a few days you will be fine and we shall take another long walk together."

But in a few days Piero was not fine. He felt nothing, not even the pain in his neck. He refused a doctor and insisted on visitors. It did not occur to him that he would never improve, and he relished the attention. The family bowed to his wishes—no doctors, plenty of visitors. Finally, after a tiring week of constant visitors to his bedside, including the captain of police, who offered every kind of assistance but was turned down, Louisa had her way. No doctors. No visitors.

The fifty-one-year-old policeman showed no signs of recovery. If anything, Piero was so tired he could hardly speak. His face was bloodless. The contrast of his black beard against the whiteness of his skin gave him the appearance of wearing a mask. His breathing became more labored. He asked to see his children and his grandchildren.

"I have nothing to give you but my medals," he told his own children after first telling them that he would soon die.

Pasquale and Lorenzo, his younger sons, who had returned home

(75)

not realizing that their father had met with an accident, each took a medal handed to them by Louisa. Rosa and Angelina refused to accept theirs, insisting between sobs that "papa would be off the bed tomorrow." Luigi had already received his medal eleven years ago, the day Angelo was born.

"For you, Luigi, my eldest son, I have nothing but talk," Piero said with some difficulty.

"Don't talk, Papa. Save your strength."

Piero insisted.

"I have lived my life as I wanted. But you," he gasped, "you are not living the life you should have. There is Madelena to think about; there are the children; the future."

"Enough, Papa. Rest."

"No. I shall finish. You are all so very young. You need opportunity. Especially Angelo. I have tried to put Naples in his heart and Italy in his soul. But I have come to see that what I am, I am. All of you must be what you must be. And what you must be cannot be found in Naples."

"No more, Papa."

Piero wheezed on with effort.

"I have done much thinking lately. Especially with all those people going to America. Angelo can tell you that. He knows. Perhaps I have been selfish. Perhaps my revolution so long ago was my revolution, not yours. I do not think things are well in our country now. Perhaps you should think of yourselves. Yes, you should think of yourselves."

Piero seemed to gather some strength. He was talking easier. For the first time in his life he was trying to face the truth. And for the first time in his life he was trying to give Luigi sensible advice. It made him stronger. Although he was not about to confess any real disappointment with the course of his life, Piero, nevertheless, was revealing some disillusionment with the way things had worked out.

"Did you know that Garibaldi lived in America, once, a long time ago, Luigi?"

"Yes, Papa. You have mentioned it."

"He liked the Americans. He often told us that. He used to say that the Americans understood real liberty and that we could learn from them. I'll tell you another thing. I called the Americans 'lunatics' because I wanted you, your sisters and your brothers to remain here, near me, near your mama. I have been afraid that you would someday leave us. The Americans are not lunatics. They are strong and smart."

"Go to sleep, Papa. You will not improve if you keep on like this."

"I am not finished, Luigi. No, the Americans are not lunatics. Once their president, Lincoln—Abraham Lincoln—wrote a letter to Garibaldi. I saw it myself. He asked Garibaldi to come back to America. And do you know why? No. You do not know why. So I shall tell you why. The Americans had a terrible war. They fought among themselves. During that war, Lincoln had need for a good general. He asked Garibaldi to be his general. Garibaldi was the best. But Garibaldi refused. He told the American president that Italy needed him more, but if it turned out that Italy did not need him, he would surely be an American general. To want someone like Garibaldi tells you something about Americans, Luigi. They are very smart. Think about that, my son. And for Garibaldi to have said what he said speaks well of America. I am proud to have served such a man. But now you have your own life to live. You cannot live mine. I did not pay attention to my children. You must not be like me. You must make plans very soon. Throw your lot in with the Americans, Luigi, before it is too late. Now I shall sleep."

If Luigi had any doubts at all about leaving Naples to seek a better future for himself, for Madelena and for his children, his father had put them to rest. Luigi knew what he had to do and he knew where he would go. America.

Two days later, Piero Capello died.

❧ *seven* ❧

It took months following the death of Piero for the family to settle down. In all the sorrow no one remembered Angelo's eleventh birthday—an event that occurred four days after the accident. Not even Angelo remembered. It went by unnoticed.

Luigi continued to keep his ideas to himself, however, biding the proper moment to discuss them with Madelena. His mother, Louisa, spent most of her time in San Liborio lighting candles to Piero's memory. The city fathers had voted to give her a small pension for as long as she would live. It was a small monthly allowance that was not quite half of Piero's meager salary. Still it was something. She would not starve.

The chief of police, who had known Piero since the old days, pushed the matter through the city council, insisting that was the least that could be done for the widow of a "Garibaldi soldier." No one dared to challenge him. The vote was unanimous. Since the house now belonged to Louisa under the terms of the "services rendered" agreement Piero had worked out years before, she now had a measure of security. But the security was hers and only hers. None of her children could inherit either the house or the pension.

The chief of police even tried to convince Luigi to become a policeman.

"You are tall enough," he told him. "You are strong enough. You are your father's son. You have a right."

Luigi refused the offer. It was a better job than that of a laborer. It paid more. Everyone had respect for a policeman. Nevertheless, Luigi rejected the idea, thinking that if he did become a policeman he would be bound to Naples for the rest of his life. But more than that. It was not so much what *his* future would amount to. What was important was the future of his children. His dying father's advice stuck in his mind like a tune that would not go away.

Angelo roamed aimlessly around the docks by himself, unable to come to terms with Piero's passing, unable to recognize his own growing restlessness.

"I am not my grandfather," he would end up muttering. "I cannot be him. I am Angelo Capello. I must be me."

And then Angelo would find a place at the edge of a broken-down, vacant dock. There he would sit in the brilliant sunshine watching the wheeling, diving gulls above and gazing at the horizon past the Island of Capri with the wonder of what lay beyond.

Luigi's moment came before the year was out. Madelena herself gave her husband the opening he prayed he would not have to make.

On one clear, star-strewn night before going to bed, Madelena casually murmured how things had changed.

"Things are not the same, Luigi, are they? Naples without papa is different, isn't it?"

"Yes, Madelena."

"We should go away from here. There is already one ghost too many."

"And leave mama, your parents, your brothers?"

"Your mama will never leave this house. You know that. As for my parents and brothers—Paolo is going to be married and he says that he is going to take his bride with him to America. Mama and papa say that they will go with them. My other brothers too! What do you think of that, Luigi?"

"What do I think of that?" Luigi's heart raced. He grabbed Madelena's hands and held them tightly. "I'll tell you what I think of that!

"I have been thinking about it for months. I have been thinking about it since long before papa died. We—he and I—even talked about it. Before papa died—two days before—he told me to consider such a thing. I tell you, Madelena, a voyage like that would not be for us as much as it would be for our children. There is opportunity in America. There are riches in America. There are . . ."

(80)

"How will we get there, Luigi? We have no money."

"There are ways. It will not be easy. But there are ways. First we have to decide that we shall do this thing, that we shall go to America. Then we'll tell mama, but not the children—not until we are ready to pack. And then we'll plan on how it shall be done. Is it settled then?"

"Is what settled?"

"That we go to America."

"Do we have to decide tonight? It is late."

"Tonight, Madelena. Tonight!"

"It would be a good thing, eh, Luigi? We are young and healthy. The children will benefit?"

"Yes. The children will benefit."

"I go wherever you go."

"Then it is settled."

"Yes, Luigi, it is settled."

❧ *eight* ❧

The warm autumn sun yielded to cooler winter months. The new year came shrouded in misty rains that dampened the crooked streets around the Piazza Carita and the rest of Naples. The old city had temporarily lost her color, her sparkle, her voice, her aroma.

Angelo continued to wander around the docks like a prowling cat, looking up at the gulls and out at the harbor, the horizon or wherever his imagination took him. He also helped his father fix streets.

Luigi was as miserable as the clammy weather. The bright future was still only a promise—no more, no less.

Before the mist had settled over Naples, Luigi had told his mother about the plans to leave Italy for America.

"What must be, must be," Louisa quietly told him and left the house to light another candle.

"We will take you with us, Mama," Luigi seemed to be pleading as he followed his mother halfway down the street.

"With what? With your father's inheritance?" she snapped. "And will you take Rosa and Angelina and Pasquale and Lorenzo, too? You make your plans, Luigi. And we shall make ours."

Half in despair and half in anger, Luigi let his equally despairing mother walk on alone. "I am a man, Mama. I shall do what I have to do," he shouted after her. Louisa did not answer. She kept on walking.

Luigi was determined more than ever to see his plan through. But for all his determination he accomplished little. He managed to save a small amount of money. Unfortunately, it was hardly enough to transport a family of nine across the Atlantic Ocean—not to mention half the Mediterranean Sea.

He did odd jobs around the docks to be close to the ships and sailors and whoever else might miraculously present him with the golden key to unlock America's golden door. Twice he had opportunities to sail away. But they were only for him and did not include the rest of the family. Both were ships in need of ordinary seamen, however inexperienced. One was a Canadian vessel returning to Halifax. The other was a British freighter bound for San Francisco by way of the Suez Canal, India, Malaya and Hawaii. Luigi was almost tempted to sign on the latter. What an adventure, he thought—go to San Francisco, get rich and then send for the entire family—everybody, including the La Starzas, Madelena's family. But Luigi was only dreaming. He knew that. He could no more go by himself than could the man in the moon swim.

The harbor became quiet as the drizzly months wore on. Few ships came and went. Those that did were usually small freighters that chugged around the Mediterranean Sea. Luigi waited for springtime when the world would come alive again.

Spring came to Naples and the city exploded with sun, life and hope. The ships came too. But none were for the Capellos. Tomasina, Maria and Giovanni all came down with the mumps—separately, Angelo, Vito, Teresa and Fausto stayed healthy. By the time the little ones had recovered, spring had turned into summer, and a frightening epidemic of cholera swept through Naples. The disease ran amok all summer long. The port was closed. No ships were allowed into the harbor. No one was allowed to leave Naples in any direction. The city and its people were devastated. Thousands died. Thousands more lay in their beds groaning. Miraculously, none of the Capellos nor any of the La Starzas came down with the disease.

"God was good to us," Louisa proclaimed. "We should pray and celebrate."

By the time the epidemic had run its course, another autumn had returned to Naples. The family prayed for their deliverance and gave thanks. They also had their celebration—Angelo's twelfth birthday—September 24, 1882. Although the port was now open to shipping, few oceangoing vessels wanted any part of Naples. They continued to stay away. Luigi was faced with another winter of frustration.

He confided in Angelo. "It is time, Angelo, that you know what we plan. We are going to America. Soon we hope."

Angelo's heart pounded with the idea that such a great adventure would soon be upon them. But his mind wrestled with the notion that somehow this would be a betrayal of his grandfather's spirit. Luigi, not knowing how strong or stubborn were the seeds of Italian pride his father, Piero, had implanted in Angelo, quickly assured Angelo that what they were about to do was right.

"Papa told me to do this thing on his deathbed. It was his dying wish that we all go to America to seek our fortunes."

Angelo was satisfied.

Luigi was able to get a better job. He became a gang boss—a foreman—of one of several work crews building a new dock. Angelo

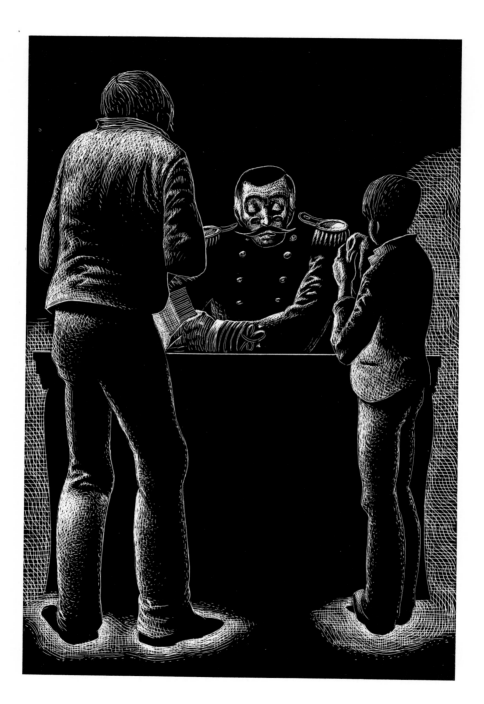

worked as a laborer in his father's crew. Eleven-year-old Vito became an apprentice in the same crew. The pay all around was better than before. The family had purpose now and their treasury improved.

Another damp winter fell on Naples. Luigi's spirit was near the breaking point. It must be this coming spring, he told himself over and over again. This coming spring or never.

"Don't worry, Papa," Angelo comforted him. "Nobody will get sick. There will be a ship for us. And we shall go to America."

In February of the new year, 1883, the chief of police summoned Luigi to his office. Luigi, not knowing why the chief wanted him and thinking perhaps he would be given a better job—he certainly had committed no crime—ran all the way in a heavy downpour. Angelo ran with him. They were ushered into the chief's office. There they stood shivering, dripping, twisting their soaking hats, unaware of the growing puddles on the floor.

Sitting behind his ornate desk, the chief seemed all business. He stroked his great mustache, leaned forward to inspect his wet floor and peered at Luigi and Angelo over the rims of his glasses. He picked up a sheet of paper and casually waved it back and forth.

"I have a letter from an old friend in America," he began. "My friend lives in New York City. You have heard of New York?"

"Yes," father and son said in unison.

"Good. He is a rich man. He is a man of many interests and much influence. Are you listening, you two?"

"Yes," they repeated again in unison.

"Good. The name of my friend is Alberto Carlo Pelozzi. Do you know such a name?"

"No."

"Mr. Pelozzi is in need of some good workers. He has asked me to find him the best. If I can do this for him, he promises to bring such men and their families to America at his expense. In return for such generosity, these men that I shall find and those of their families who are able to work will serve Mr. Pelozzi in whatever way is suitable and honorable for a period of not less than seven years. During that period Mr. Pelozzi will attend to all of their needs."

Luigi stared down at the letter on the desk, wondering how the chief profited from these arrangements. It didn't matter, however. This was the chance he had been waiting for.

"Do you still wish to go to America, Luigi Capello?"

Luigi continued to stare at the letter. Angelo looked at his father and then at the chief. His eyes widened with expectation.

"Are you listening, Luigi? Do you still wish to go to America?"

"Yes," he whispered. "Yes, yes, yes. A thousand times yes."

"Good," replied the chief. "However, you must be patient. You and your family will not leave tomorrow. I must choose others. In two or three months' time an agent for Mr. Pelozzi will arrive in Naples. He will talk to you and he will have papers for you to sign. He will return to America. You and your family will go with him."

⇘ *nine* ⇙

On April 18, Luigi and Madelena Capello and their seven children stood on American "soil" for the first time—the teak deck of the S.S. *Baltimore City*. From there they looked down at the crowd of friends and relatives who had come to say *addio*—good-bye—to the 151 emigrants on board.

Madelena had no difficulty seeing her parents and brothers. Louisa Capello stood with them, motionless. They all stood in the center of the crowd. They did not wave. They did not smile. Neither did Madelena, Luigi nor any of the children. All of them were frozen in silent stares. It would be ten years before Madelena would see any of her family again. They would all come to America as they said they would.

Luigi looked in vain for his sisters. They were nowhere to be seen. For weeks they pleaded with him not to go. They accused Luigi of cruelty for leaving them to an uncertain fate. There was little he could do to console them except to wish that they would marry soon. Luigi hoped by some miracle his brothers would appear, but they had gone north again to find work. Luigi would never see any of them again—not his sisters, not his brothers, not his mother.

At precisely 7:00 P.M., the bow and stern lines were cast off. The S.S. *Baltimore City* began to glide through the smooth and gentle waters of the Bay of Naples. She headed due west toward the blood-red setting sun and the open sea.

Angelo and Vito were too high with excitement to give much thought to the immensity of the sad farewell they had just witnessed. They raced aft to watch Naples slip away, not once thinking that it was slipping from their sight forever. Luigi was right behind them. The three of them stood quietly at the rail and marvelled at the sparkling, sunlit spectacle that was once their city.

Luigi was numb. Here was the reality of his longtime dream. He was on a ship bound for America with his wife and children. But leaving the land of his father, his mother and all those Capellos and Paolis who had come before him left him striken with guilt and remorse instead of the happiness he thought he would feel. It seemed to Luigi that he and his family had lived in Italy since time began. And now, he, Luigi Capello, was the first to break the bond.

He shoved his hand into his jacket pocket and clutched the medal his father had given to him so many years before—the medal for bravery. Softly he began to sing,

Addio, addio, Napoli,
Addio, addio . . .

(87)

But his voice trailed off as tears rolled out of his eyes. The joy and sadness were indistinguishable. He turned around and walked back to where he had left Madelena and the rest of their children. Vito trailed after him.

Angelo alone remained at the rail, until the city became a blur. He was unable to believe that he was going to see, finally, what lay over the horizon past Capri. He heard someone calling. It was Vito.

"Angelo. Angelo."

IV

Endings

May 7, 1944

Monday

≽ *one* ≼

"Angelo? Angelo!"

The old priest put his palsied hand on Angelo's shoulder. He shook him a little.

"It's me, Angelo. Vito. Your brother. Do you remember?"

"Eh? Ah, Vito. Where have you been? I have been waiting for you for hours. Do I remember what?"

"Never mind. I have been here for ten minutes and you didn't even notice me. What have you been staring at in that painting of yours?"

"Oh. That. You know how it is, Vito."

"No, Angelo. I do not know how it is. And what's more I cannot remember how it was. I see you have heard from Vinny. He is well?"

"Yes. He is fine."

"Thank God. Now let's go home. I have a wedding to perform tomorrow. Do you remember?"

≽ *two* ≼

April 18 had always been a traditional day at the Capellos. From the first April 18 the family spent in New York through all the April 18s that followed—most of them in New Haven, Connecticut, where Luigi moved his family when his service for the *padrone*, Signor Pelozzi, had ended—Luigi never forgot to celebrate their departure from Naples. Three weeks later he would celebrate May 7, their arrival in America. This he did without fail by drinking a toast to the occasions with a glass of Lacrima Christi, a glorious dry red wine made from the grapes that grew on the slopes of Mount Vesuvius.

When Luigi finally died in 1935, at age eighty-five, he had lived long enough to see his dreams for his children become a reality.

Angelo prospered the most, as a building contractor and restaurateur. Vito, who never married, gave up a thriving hat-manufacturing business in Danbury, Connecticut, to become a priest. That was in 1921. He was ordained four years later, at age fifty. Teresa married a physician, had several children and lived a happy social life in Boston. Fausto died during the great flu epidemic in 1918. He left his wife and son comfortably fixed from the proceeds of a profitable laundry business. Tomasina married a Canadian businessman. They had five children. She still lives in Toronto. Maria married a Bridgeport plumber who became wealthy manufacturing brass fittings for other plumbers. Giovanni, the youngest, served in the U.S. Army during the Spanish-American War. He went to Cuba, caught yellow fever and survived. He married, never had children and spent his life selling automobiles, bicycles and wagons.

Madelena, who outlived Luigi by two years, had the best of all the worlds. She took great pride in the material accomplishment of her family, and had the singular good fortune of not only being surrounded by Capellos but by her own mother and father and the families of her brothers. On the day Luigi passed on, Madelena gave herself full credit for having had the foresight to come to America, without which none of them would have ever reached such prosperous heights.

In any event, following his father's death, Angelo continued his father's ritual of celebrating their days of departure and arrival.

"*Alla salute!*"

In recent years, Angelo had added a few touches of his own. With a great symbolic flourish, he would tip his glass of Lacrima Christi before the painting of the Bay of Naples. That was on April 18. On the following May 7, he would stage a great feast in Ristorante Capello—on the house. At the height of the festivities, he would bang

an empty wine bottle or water tumbler for quiet, ceremoniously plant a small American flag in the center of the table directly in front of the painting, and with his back to the Bay of Naples he would toast their arrival once more.

There was no toast this past April 18, 1944, however. Angelo had closed the restaurant late in January. Sixty years of Capello ceremonies had abruptly come to a halt. The marriage of his granddaughter, Angelina Palmieri, to Private First Class Louis Bianchi from San Francisco last October was the final ceremony so far as Angelo was concerned.

Now, on this May 7, 1944, Angelo sat alone in the gloomy and cavernous restaurant brooding over the past and contemplating the few years that remained to him. One year from this very day the war in Europe would end. Germany would surrender. Millions of soldiers still alive would have a new lease on life—a new beginning. But for Angelo, the war had ended last January.

Before him on the table was a framed photograph of Vinny and a framed document. Angelo had come to the restaurant this afternoon to hang the photograph and the document next to the two Roosevelt letters. It was to be his last gesture before leaving the restaurant for good. In his pocket was his grandfather's medal for bravery, the same medal given to his own father, Luigi, who in turn passed it on to him. Angelo had hoped someday to give it to Vinny. But now that would never happen. Vinny was dead.

"I have paid my bill," Angelo muttered to himself.

He removed the medal from his pocket and placed it on the photograph of his son. It seemed to satisfy him, somehow. Presently, Angelo rose, found a hammer and a couple of nails. He hung the two framed pieces next to the Roosevelt letters. He taped the medal to the top of the framed photograph. Angelo stepped back and looked at the wall. The document was crooked. He straightened it. For the hundreth time or more he read it with profound disbelief:

(97)

IN GRATEFUL MEMORY OF
Theodore Vincent Capello
Major, Army of the United States
WHO DIED IN THE SERVICE
OF HIS COUNTRY AT
Anzio, Italy
January 24, 1944
HE STANDS IN THE UNBROKEN LINE OF
PATRIOTS WHO HAVE DARED TO DIE
THAT FREEDOM MIGHT LIVE AND GROW
AND INCREASE ITS BLESSINGS
FREEDOM LIVES AND THROUGH IT HE LIVES
IN A WAY THAT HUMBLES THE
UNDERTAKING OF MOST MEN
Franklin D. Roosevelt
PRESIDENT OF THE UNITED STATES OF AMERICA

Vinny was buried in the American Military Cemetery at Nettuno, Italy, in the land of his fathers. He was the first of the Capellos to have returned.

In a brief instant, Angelo conjured up the image of his grandfather, Piero. Piero, that solemn, self-indulgent old soldier who offered his poor life for liberty and managed to survive to live in his own way. There was something of Piero in Vinny. No. They were each other. They were one and the same mixed in the soil of Italy, joined together after their sixty-three-year separation—great-grandfather, great-grandson. One an Italian, the other an American. Both proud and harmless men who believed in the contagion of their own freedom and were done in by their innocence.

Angelo went down the rickety steps to his wine celler. He returned with a bottle of Lacrima Christi. He poured a half glass and tipped it in the direction of the photograph with its taped medal.

(99)

"To you, grandfather Piero. To you, Vinny, my son. *Salute!*"

Angelo set the partially filled glass on the counter and walked out of Ristorante Capello for the last time.

Addio.